THIS CANDLEWICK BOOK BELONGS TO:

For my granddaughter Isobel
P.L.

For Francesco
A.G.

First U.S. paperback edition 1996

The Library of Congress has cataloged the hardcover edition as follows:

Lively, Penelope, 1933 –
Good night, sleep tight / Penelope Lively ; illustrated by Adriano Gon.—1st U.S. ed.
Summary: A girl's stuffed animals, Frog, Lion, and Cat, and her doll, Mary Ann,
each take her on a different bedtime adventure.
ISBN 1-56402-417-2 (hardcover)
[1. Bedtime—Fiction. 2. Toys—Fiction.] I. Gon, Adriano, ill. II. Title.
PZ7.L7397Gf 1995
[E]—dc20 94-1600
ISBN 1-56402-831-3 (paperback)

2 4 6 8 10 9 7 5 3 1

Printed in Hong Kong

This book was typeset in M Garamond.
The pictures were done with emulsion paints.

Candlewick Press
2067 Massachusetts Avenue
Cambridge, Massachusetts 02140

Good Night, Sleep Tight

by
Penelope Lively

illustrated by
Adriano Gon

CANDLEWICK PRESS
CAMBRIDGE, MASSACHUSETTS

There was once a girl who had a large family.

All day long she took
care of everybody.
She was rushed off her feet.

She washed and
shopped and cooked.

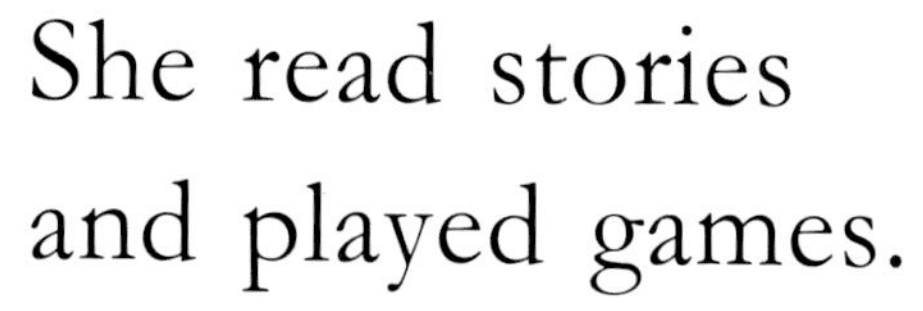

She read stories
and played games.

Sometimes
she got annoyed.

Other times she said she was worn
to a frazzle and she must have a
few minutes of peace and quiet.

And at the end of the day
she washed their faces

and brushed their teeth
and combed their hair.

She read them a last story
and then took them
off to bed.

"Good night," said the girl. "Sleep tight."
And they all settled down to sleep.

"Who's kicking?" said the girl. "Who's whispering? Who's jiggling around?"
Lion said, "We have an idea."
The girl said, "We go to sleep now.
We don't have ideas."
Frog said, "We want to take you on adventures—one adventure for each of us."
"I will have to think about this," said the girl.
"Please," they all said. "Please."

So the girl said that if they promised to go straight off to sleep afterward they could each take her on an adventure.

"Me first," said Frog. "I'm going to take you to the place where I live."

"You live here," said the girl, "in my house."

"Sometimes I do, and sometimes I don't. Sometimes I live at the bottom of the pond. The pond is where I do frog things," said Frog. "You can do them with me."

"I do deep diving.
I do fast swimming.
I do enormous jumping."

"More!" said the girl. "Again!"

"That's all for now," said Frog. "It's someone else's turn."

And they swam up out of the pond and *plop!* back into bed again.

"I go to a faraway place," said Lion. "Only I know where it is.

I roar and I shout and I sing. You can join in. Nobody tells you to stop making so much noise because there's nobody there."

They howled and they squealed and
they screamed. They made such a racket
that the ground shivered and
the stars shook.

"Louder!" shouted the girl.
They shrieked until
the leaves whirled and
the trees fell down.

"That'll do," said Lion.
"Let's have quiet now."
And back to bed they went.

"I go walking in the night," said Cat.
"Come on . . ."

"I go into the dark world
and I see things. I'm not afraid."
"Am I afraid?" asked the girl.
"No. You can see things too.
The world is huge and dark and
exciting. We go hunting
for surprises."
"Oooh . . . !" said the girl.
"Aaah . . . ! What's that!"

"That's enough surprises," said Cat.
And they came out of the dark and into the warm bed again.

"Me now," said Mary Ann. "Hurry up! We're going to the party."
"I don't have a party dress," said the girl.
"Yes, you do," said Mary Ann. "Look! And here are all my friends. Now they're your friends too."

"I don't know how to dance like that," said the girl.

"Yes, you do. Try. That's it—one, two, three. One, two, three."

And they danced and danced. They danced till they dropped, and then the girl said, "My feet hurt and I'm sleepy."

"Time to go home," said Mary Ann.
"I'm too tired to walk," said the girl.
"You don't have to," said Mary Ann.
"Look where we are."

And the girl looked,
and there she was
in her own bed.
And there beside her
were Frog and Lion
and Cat and Mary Ann.
"Okay," said the girl.
"Everybody settle down now.
We've had our adventures, and
it's time to sleep. Good night, sleep tight."
"Good night," they said.
"And if you're very good," said the girl,
"if you're very good and go straight to sleep,
and if you're good all day tomorrow,
we just might do it again one night."

Penelope Lively is a celebrated novelist for adults, though she began her writing career with novels for children. Inspired by the birth of her first grandchild in 1988, she returned to children's literature with *The Cat, the Crow, and the Banyan Tree*, her first picture book ever. The idea for *Good Night, Sleep Tight* came, she says, "as I listened to my granddaughter talking to her toys and remembered talking to my own toys as a child."

Adriano Gon illustrated *Good Night, Sleep Tight* with very small drawings that he photographed and enlarged. He then painted the colors directly on the developed film. "I really enjoyed using this technique," he says. "It makes the pictures very flat and very bright." Adriano Gon lives in Italy.
